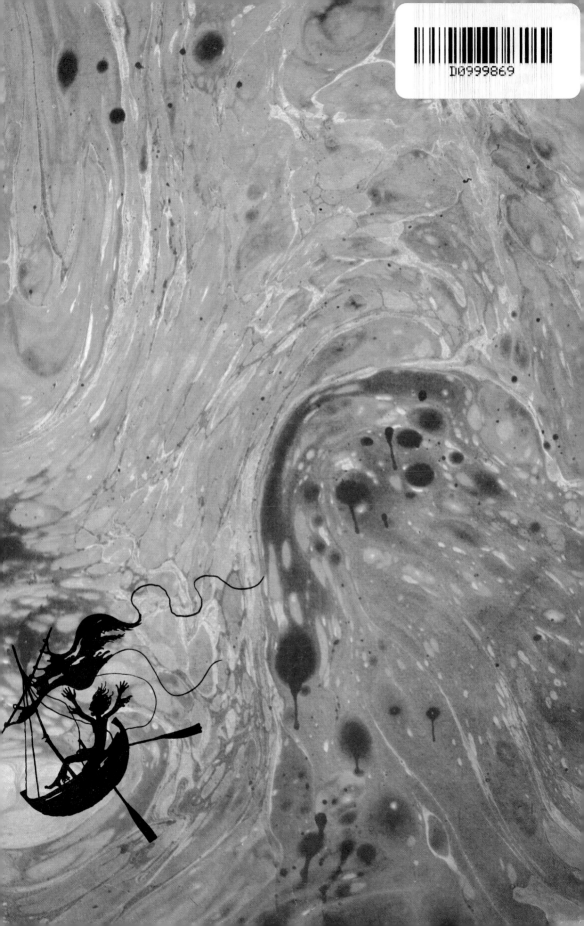

THE KINGDOM
UNDER
THE SEA
and other stories

THE **K**INGDOM
UNDER
THE
SEA

and other stories

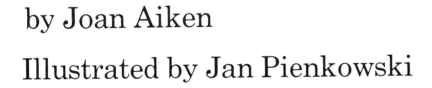

by Joan Aiken

Illustrated by Jan Pienkowski

JONATHAN CAPE   THIRTY BEDFORD SQUARE   LONDON

FIRST PUBLISHED 1971
REPRINTED 1975
TEXT © 1971 BY JOAN AIKEN
ILLUSTRATIONS © 1971 BY JAN PIENKOWSKI

JONATHAN CAPE LTD, 30 BEDFORD SQUARE, LONDON WC1

ISBN 0 224 61882 2

'The Sun-God's Castle', 'The Sun's Cousin'
and 'The Kingdom Under the Sea' are based on
stories contained in *Croatian Tales of Long Ago*
by Ivana Berlic-Mazuranic, translated by
F. S. Copeland (Allen & Unwin, London, 1924).

PRINTED IN GREAT BRITAIN BY FLETCHER & SON LTD, NORWICH
BOUND BY RICHARD CLAY (THE CHAUCER PRESS) LTD
BUNGAY, SUFFOLK

CONTENTS

THE KINGDOM UNDER THE SEA

Once a fisherman lived on the lonely shore. Every day he went out to sea in his little boat and caught fish; every night he cooked and ate the fish; so he lived.

At last he said to himself, "Even the birds of the air and the fish of the sea have a better life than I, for at least they have companions. I will pray to Zora-djevojka, the Dawn Maiden, to bring some comfort into my life."

So he rowed out to sea in his little boat, and for three days he neither ate nor fished, but let the tides carry him where they would. On the third morning he saw Zora-djevojka, the Dawn Maiden, the Sun's beloved daughter, coming swiftly over the waves in her silver boat. She looked upon the fisherman with kindness.

"What grieves you, my son? Why do you look so sad?"

"Oh, Zora-djevojka, beautiful Dawn Maiden! Won't you please bring a bit of comfort and cheerfulness into my life?"

"Well," said the Dawn Maiden, "for three days you have spared my fishes, so I will help you. Go home to your hut on the lonely shore and wait for what fortune will come to you."

So she sank beneath the waves in her silver boat, and the fisherman rowed home. When he reached his hut on the lonely shore, there was a poor ragged girl sitting outside the door.

"My parents have died and I have come to be your wife," she told the fisherman.

"Is *this* all the fortune the Dawn Maiden has sent me?" he thought, but there was nothing to be done; he took her for his wife. And he thought again, "Maybe she has rich kinsfolk who will come presently with gold and marriage-gifts."

But nothing of that sort happened and matters went on as before. Every day the fisherman went out in his boat and caught fish, while his wife wove nets of hemp; every night they ate the fish, with wild herbs and roots which the wife gathered on the cliffside. But after they had eaten she would take his head in her lap and comb his hair, or she would play sweet tunes on her pair of bone pipes. And she told him wonderful tales, about the sea-king's palace, about the windswept isle of Bujan and the amber stone Alatyr, about Perun, the god of the thunder, about the dragon of Lake Rikavatz and the Zmayevska Vatra, the dragons' fire, which lies deep down below the round of the world. And the fisherman was comforted, for he thought, "Maybe she is really a fairy-wife that the Dawn Maiden sent me. Maybe in the course of time she will show me all these marvels."

Weeks went by and months went by; in the course of time they had a little son. And every day the fisherman went fishing, and every night the wife told her tales.

But one night the fisherman became angry, and he said, "I will wait no longer. Tomorrow you must show me one of these marvels! Take me to the sea-king's palace and show me his throne of silver, and his trumpets of pearl, and his coral candles burning beneath the waves!"

Then his wife was frightened, and she said, "It is only a tale that I told you to ease your heart. I am just a poor girl; what do I know of the sea-king's palace? How can I take you there?"

But the fisherman would not listen to her. He said, "Tomorrow at dawn you must go out along the shore and find the way to the sea-king's palace. And if you cannot find it, do not trouble to return, for you will not be welcome."

So the next morning at dawn the poor wife took her baby in her arms and set out along the shore. All day she walked, and never a soul did she see, let alone the way to the sea-king's palace. At nightfall she was tired and lay down to rest. She fell asleep, and when she woke, her baby was gone!

All next day she called and she hunted, but no trace of her baby could she discover, not so much as a footprint on the sand. So on the third day she turned homeward, for what else could she do? By the time she reached the hut her hair had turned white and she had gone dumb with grieving, so she could tell her husband nothing of what had happened.

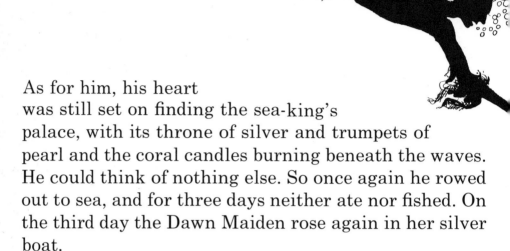

As for him, his heart
was still set on finding the sea-king's
palace, with its throne of silver and trumpets of
pearl and the coral candles burning beneath the waves.
He could think of nothing else. So once again he rowed
out to sea, and for three days neither ate nor fished. On
the third day the Dawn Maiden rose again in her silver
boat.

"What troubles you now, my son?"

"Oh, Zora-djevojka, beautiful Dawn Maiden, won't
you please show me the way to the sea-king's palace?"

"Very well," she said. "I will help you this time, but
no more. At the next new moon get into your boat and
let the wind carry you eastwards until you reach the
windswept isle of Bujan, the sun's bright home, where
shines the amber stone Alatyr, guarded by the eldest
brother of all the crows. There I will tell you what to do
next."

So the fisherman went home. He said nothing to his
wife, but at the next new moon got into his boat and let
the wind carry him eastwards until he reached the
windswept isle of Bujan, where the grass grows green
and the grapes hang on the wild vines. And there Zora-
djevojka the Dawn Maiden was waiting for him.

"Do you see that mill-wheel floating in the waves, my son, with the mermaids playing round it? You must ask the mermaids to turn the wheel, and whirl you down to the sea-king's halls. But mind, once you are down there, you will not be able to return, for three terrible guardians bar the way back to earth!"

"Oh, thank you, beautiful Dawn Maiden, but once I am down there I shan't wish to come back to earth!"

So the fisherman rowed along to where the mermaids were playing round the mill-wheel.

"Dear mermaids, won't you please turn the wheel and spin me down to the sea-king's palace?"

So the mermaids spun the wheel until there was a great funnel-hole in the sea, and the fisherman's boat went riding down to the sea-king's palace. He saw the silver throne, the burning candles of coral, and the sea-people blowing on trumpets of pearl. There was the great sea-king himself, with his tangled beard and his horns and his ruby eyes. And there, too, was the fisherman's little son, lying in a golden cradle.

Well, when the fisherman saw his baby son, all thoughts about the splendour of the sea-king's palace went clean out of his head.

"How dared they steal my little son and bring him down here?" he thought. "And how in the world am I going to get him home?"

Now, while this had been happening to the fisherman, his poor dumb wife was left alone in the lonely hut. So what did she do? Every night she cooked the fisherman's supper, in case he should come back, and every day she wove nets of hemp. Then, since the fisherman did not come home, every morning she took his supper to the cliffside and fed it to the wild snakes; every noon she took the hempen nets and gave them to the sea-birds to build their nests.

Weeks went by and months went by, and still the fisherman did not return. But his boat came floating back, upside down. So the wife took her bone pipes and a bone fish-hook, she stepped into the boat and put out to sea. And the wind carried her to a distant place where there are three caverns of cloud: in one is a dreadful dragon, in one a fearsome bird, and in one a monstrous bee.

The wife came to the first cavern and saw the dreadful dragon, stretched out all along the sea, shooting out foam and spume from her nostrils, lashing up the waves with her tail. The wife dared not go by, but took out her pipes and played on them. Directly she did so, all the snakes in the world came swimming.

"Let the woman pass by your cave, dragon mother! She has done us many a kindness and fed us every morning."

"Very well," said the dragon. "But only this once, mind!"

So she let the woman's boat pass by.

Next the wife came to the second cavern, where there sat a fearsome bird, large as a mountain; her feathers were of brass and her beak of iron. When she clapped her wings, the hurricane blew. But the woman played a soft tune on her pipes. Directly she did so, all the birds in the world came flying.

"Do let the woman go by, O mother of all the birds! Every day she has given us hemp for our nests."

"Very well," said the bird. "But only this once!"

So she let the boat pass by.

Now the woman came to the third cave, where lived the great bee. When it buzzed, the lightning flashed and the thunder pealed. But the wife caught the bee in her sleeve. With the bee in her sleeve she rowed on, into the unknown sea beyond, and she let down her little bone hook on its slender line.

It was just at this moment that the fisherman was trying to escape from the sea-king's palace, struggling, with the golden cradle in his arms, to swim up through the great weight of sea that lay like a dome above. And as he struggled to swim, the woman's little bone hook caught in his hair and pulled him up. She drew both father and child to the top of the sea, and when she saw them a spring of joy burst in her heart and the power of speech returned to her.

"Oh, my husband! My little son, that I never hoped to see again!"

So she helped them into the boat and they embraced one another.

But now all the people of the sea came in chase—the mermaids with their blue stone eyes, the foam spirits with their long white fingers, and the great horned sea-king himself. Huge waves rose, and the wind howled. And they still had to get past the dreadful dragon and the fearsome bird.

In his terror the fisherman called to the Dawn Maiden.

"Oh, Zora-djevojka, beautiful Dawn Maiden, do help me just once more!"

The Dawn Maiden came in her silver boat, skimming over the waves.

"I said I would not help you again," she told the fisherman.

But on the woman she looked kindly, and she said, "O faithful wife, to you I will give help!" And she gave the wife a silken kerchief. Quickly they spread it out, and it became a sail; the boat flew over the waves, faster than the sea-people could follow. It flew past the dragon's cave, and past the fearsome bird. As they passed the third cave, the golden bee flew out of the woman's sleeve, and they saw the lightning flash and heard the thunder crack behind them. But the boat flew on, reached the shore, split on a rock, and sank. They waded ashore just below their lonely hut.

From that day on, every evening to the end of his life, the fisherman ate his fish and his wild herbs in contentment; never again did he wish to visit the sea-king's palace.

THE IMPRISONED QUEEN

Once there were three brothers, kings, who decided to build a city and call it Skadar. They chose a spot by a river, on the side of a mountain, they called three hundred workmen together, and for three years they toiled at building the city.

But what happened? Every night a vila—a wicked fairy who lived in the clouds and mist up at the top of the mountain—caused the whole hillside to tremble and heave so that the walls fell down, the stones fell apart, and all their work was to do again.

At the end of three years they were no further on.

When the fourth year was beginning the vila called down from her hiding-place in the clouds and mist.

"Kings! You will never build your city of Skadar until you find a twin brother and sister, Stoja and Stojane.

You must tie them together and bury them under the great gate of the city. Then the walls will stand firm, the stones will cling together, and the buildings will not fall down at night."

King Voukashan, the eldest of the three brothers, had a faithful servant, Desimir. To this man he entrusted six wagonloads of treasure, and sent him off to wander over the whole wide world, looking for a twin brother and sister, Stoja and Stojane.

"Find them," he told Desimir, "buy them for slaves, trick them or kidnap them, but bring them back somehow so that we can bury them under the great gate and build our city of Skadar."

Desimir set out with his six wagonloads of treasure, and was gone for three years. At the end of that time he came back again.

"I have searched through the whole wide world," he told King Voukashan. "Not a town or a village have I missed, but nowhere have I found a twin boy and girl named Stoja and Stojane. So here are your six wagonloads of treasure back again, King Voukashan."

Now the truth of the matter was that Desimir had found Stoja and Stojane the very first day after he had left the king: a beautiful youth and girl living not far from the fairy's mountain. He spent the night at their hut, they gave him soft water to wash in, bread and salt, and a clean, sweet bed. Next morning he thought, "What have they done that they should be buried under the great gate of the city?" So he said nothing to them, but went off and wandered about the world for three years, and then returned to King Voukashan.

The three brothers went on trying to build their town of Skadar, and every night the stones fell apart and the buildings fell down. Then the vila, the wicked fairy, called down from her hiding-place in the clouds and mist:

"Kings! Each one of you is married to a wife. Whichever of those three wives takes food tomorrow to the workmen building the walls of the city, that one must be walled up in one of the pillars of the great gate. Then the buildings will stand firm, the stones will cling together, and you will be able to build your city of Skadar."

The three brothers were not very happy about this. Not one of them wanted to lose his wife. But King Voukashan said,

"We are in the fairy's power. We must agree not to speak of this matter to our wives. Promise, my brothers! And whichever of our wives takes the workmen their food tomorrow, that one must be walled up in the great gate."

In the end his two brothers agreed. They promised not to speak to their wives of what the fairy had said. But two of them, King Voukashan and his next brother, broke their word and told their wives. Only the youngest brother, Goiko, kept his word and said nothing of the matter to his wife.

So the next morning the queen, King Voukashan's wife, said to her sister-in-law, "Oh, my sister, dear friend, I feel so ill! My head aches as if it would split in two! Be a kind sister and take the men their food today for me."

The next brother's wife said she would do this. But she, in her turn, went to the youngest brother's wife and said, "Oh, my dear friend, my sister, I have such a pain

in my arm and back! Be a kind sister and take the men their food for me today."

The youngest queen, Goiko's wife, said, "Willingly will I do this for you, but what about my little boy, little Jovo? I have not yet given him his dinner. Nor have I washed my linen and hung it out to dry."

"Do not trouble your head about that, we will do it for you."

So Goiko's young wife took the workmen their food. When her husband saw her coming his heart was wrung with anguish, but the two older brothers, without wasting a moment, seized her, tied her hands, and pushed her into a gap in the wall. Masons raised a barrier of stones in front of her. At first Goiko's wife laughed, thinking this must be a joke; then she began to cry.

"Let me out! Let me out!"

"No, you must stay there," said King Voukashan, "or we shall never build our town of Skadar."

Then Goiko's wife begged the master-mason, "At least leave a small gap, so that I can see my son Jovo when he passes by."

So, unknown to King Voukashan, this was done. And every morning Jovo passed by and called, "Are you there, my mother?" And Goiko's wife replied, "Yes, my son. Here I am!" And the stream of her tears ran by day and night.

Time went by, and Goiko died of grief. None of his uncles and aunts would look after the little Jovo, so the kindly brother and sister took him in, Stoja and Stojane. But when he was a man grown he returned again to the city of Skadar, and the place where his

mother was imprisoned.

He called, "Are you there, my mother?"

"Yes, my son. Here I am!"

Then Jovo with his club knocked down the wall and let out his mother, and they wept and embraced and he took her far away.

But the fairy, the vila, looking down from her hiding-place in the clouds and mist, saw that Goiko's wife had escaped. Angered by this, she shook the mountain until the city of Skadar fell in ruins. And it was not rebuilt for a hundred years.

But where the queen's tears flowed down the wall, a little stream runs to this day.

BABA YAGA'S DAUGHTER

There was once a girl called Vasilissa whose mother had died, and whose father married again. The second wife and her two daughters hated Vasilissa because she was so pretty and obedient, because her father loved her best, and, above all, because she was much more skilful than they at making lace, at spinning, and at knitting stockings. So her life was an unhappy one. She had to do all the work of the house, dig the garden, fetch the wood, fill the water-jugs at the village well, and make sure the hearth-stone was hot.

One time the father was away on business, and the stepmother went out to a harvest festival. Before she left, she gave each of the three girls her task for the evening: one was to make lace, one to knit stockings, and Vasilissa was to spin. The mother put out all the fires in the house, and left only one candle burning. But, in secret, she told her daughters to blow the candle out after she had gone. And this they did.

"Now what shall we do?" they said. "There is no light and our work is not done. We must get a light from the Baba Yaga."

"I shan't go," said one of the stepsisters, "for I can knit in the dark."

"I shan't go," said the other stepsister, "for I can see by the light of my needles."

Then they both said to Vasilissa, "You must go and get light from Baba Yaga!" And they turned her out of the house.

Now this Baba Yaga lived in a hut in the forest, and it was said that she ate men up as if they were chickens. So Vasilissa crossed herself and went trembling among the trees. As she felt her way forward, suddenly a knight on horseback galloped past her. He was dressed all in white, and his horse was white, and even his reins; and as he passed it grew light. Vasilissa went a little farther, and a second horseman passed; his horse and saddle were red, and his clothes, and even his reins; when he had passed by, the sun rose. Vasilissa went on. And another horseman passed by who was all in black—his cloak, his horse, and his reins; and night fell again.

Now Vasilissa came to the clearing where Baba Yaga's hut stood: the fence round the hut was made of human bones, and on the fenceposts there were skulls, glaring out of their eye-sockets. And instead of the gate there were feet, instead of bolts there were hands, instead of the lock there was a mouth with sharp teeth. And inside the fence there was a little hut standing on a cock's foot and turning round and round.

Vasilissa went stony cold with fear, for the eyes in all the skulls glared at her, but she walked forward to the hut and called out, "Hut! Stand still as you should, with your back to the wood."

At that the hut stood still, and the door opened, and a girl looked out. She was knitting a cloth with gold and silver thread. She greeted Vasilissa with a friendly smile, and exclaimed,

"Oh, my darling, my sister! I am so happy to see you, for here I pass my days all alone. I shall be glad to give you rest and refreshment as long as my mother is not here. But when she comes back, woe to us both, she will eat you up!"

When she heard this Vasilissa was even more frightened, but she said, "Oh, my sister, let me in I beg you, for I have been sent to fetch a little fire."

"Well, I will let you in," said Baba Yaga's daughter, "and we will think what is best to be done."

So she let in Vasilissa, set her by the fire, and gave her food. The two girls were very happy together; they sewed, they knitted, they talked, they laughed, and they combed their hair.

Suddenly they heard a terrible noise outside in the forest. The tree-branches creaked and the dry leaves rattled, for Baba Yaga was flying back over the trees in her pestle and mortar.

Quick as a flash, Baba Yaga's daughter turned her visitor into a needle, stuck her into the birch-broom, and set her on one side. Baba Yaga came in, and her eyes were gleaming like coals of fire. Her legs were of wood, and her nose was so large that it touched the ceiling. She stretched her jaws beyond measure.

"Tell me, my little one, my daughter, why do I smell human bones?"

"Mother, an old man came past who wanted a drink of water."

"Why did you not keep him?"

"Mother, he was old and tough; you would not have enjoyed eating him."

So Baba Yaga lay down and slept. Some hours later, out she went again, flying in her mortar and rowing it with the pestle. For it was day, and the glimmer in the skulls' eyes had dimmed. Then her daughter ran quickly and let Vasilissa out of the birch-broom, and, as before, the two girls sewed, talked, laughed, and combed their hair.

"Tell me, my sister," said Vasilissa, "who was the white knight that passed me in the forest?"

"He was the bright day."

"And who was the horseman all in red?"

"That was the red sun."

"And who was the horseman all in black?"

"That was the dark night. They are all three my mother's servants."

Then they heard a terrible whistling and crackling in the forest: Baba Yaga was returning. So her daughter made haste and turned Vasilissa into a needle once more, and stuck her into the birch-broom. Baba Yaga came in, her eyes gleaming like red coals.

"Daughter, my little darling, why does the house smell so of human bones?"

"Two old men passed by and wanted to warm their hands. I tried to make them stay, but they would not."

"Next time, be sure you make them stay," said Baba
Yaga, and then she lay down and was soon snoring.
Next morning, when the glimmer in the skulls' eyes had
died away, she went off as before, flying in her mortar
and rowing it with the pestle.

Then her daughter made haste and let Vasilissa out of
the broom. The girls set to work, sewed, talked, laughed,
and combed their hair. But they forgot how time was
flying by, and suddenly Baba Yaga stood before them.
She seized Vasilissa and cried,

"Daughter, my little one, heat the oven quickly!
Make it very hot!"

There was nothing for it. The daughter had to bring
in logs of oak and pine, light the stove, and heat up the
oven. Then Baba Yaga took her broad wooden shovel
and said to Vasilissa,

"Sit on the shovel, dear child!"

Vasilissa did not dare disobey. But she stuck her feet out sideways so that they came against the wall of the hearth.

"Not like that, my little one!"

"How, then, Baba Yaga?" And Vasilissa stuck her feet out on the other side.

"Will you sit still, girl!"

But Vasilissa could not seem to understand how Baba Yaga meant her to sit. At last the witch became angry, and said,

"You are simply wasting time! See, you must sit like this."

Down she sat on the shovel with her knees up to her chin. The two girls instantly shot her into the oven and shut the door; took their knitting, their comb and brush, and ran out of the hut. As they passed through the gate, Vasilissa took one of the skulls. Then they ran and they ran, but when they looked back, Baba Yaga had managed to burst her way out of the oven, and was running after them, calling out, "Hoo! Hoo! Hoo!"

So the girls threw the hairbrush behind them, and at once a dense thicket grew up. It took Baba Yaga a long time to struggle through the bushes, but at last she did so and came after them as before, crying, "Hoo! Hoo! Hoo!"

Then they threw the comb behind them. A thick dark oak forest grew up, and before she could fight her way through it, Baba Yaga had to tear up each tree with her teeth. But at last she came out on the other side and ran after them as before, calling out, "Hoo! Hoo! Hoo!"

Then they threw the piece of gold-and-silver knitted

cloth behind. And it turned to a great marsh. Baba Yaga started to cross it, but she sank, first up to her knees, then to her waist, then to her chin. Then she sank out of sight and was never seen again.

The two girls ran on until they came to Vasilissa's home. There was no light in the window, so Vasilissa knocked and went in.

"There you are!" said her stepsisters. "Why have you been so long? Ever since you went away we have been unable to get the fire to burn; even if we borrowed a light from the neighbours it went out as soon as we brought it in."

"Perhaps *your* fire may burn," said the stepmother.

So Vasilissa brought in the skull. But the fire from its eyes darted out and burned the stepmother and stepsisters to cinders. Then Vasilissa buried the skull in the earth, and called in Baba Yaga's daughter, and the two girls lived together happily, sewing, talking, laughing, and combing their hair.

THE SUN-GOD'S CASTLE

Once an old man lived in the forest with his three grandsons, Martin, Mihal, and Yanek. They looked after the shrine of the sun-god, the great Daybog, and kept the sacred fire burning before it.

On a fine spring morning the three grandsons got up early and went out to look at the bee-hives which they kept in the forest. It was still dark and cold, so, to raise their spirits, they sang a hymn to the sun-god, the great Daybog, calling on him to rise and give them warmth and light. They had not gone very far when a great brightness showed over the mountains beyond the forest, and suddenly in front of them they saw a beautiful young man, all dressed in gold, with a scarlet lining to his cloak. They were dazzled by him and shut their eyes.

"Well, boys! You asked me to come, but now I am here you don't seem very pleased to see me!"

So they uncovered their eyes again and peered at the sun-god through their lashes.

"What shall I do for you?" he said. "Shall I show you what lies ahead of you?"

"Yes, please, your worship!"

So he caught them up in his cloak and carried them to the top of the mountain, and there he showed them all the treasures and towns and palaces that were in the world. Next he showed them all the armies and warriors and weapons in the world. And lastly he showed them the stars and the clouds and the moon and all the winds of heaven. The brothers were quite amazed and distracted with all they saw.

At last the sun-god put them down again, back in the forest where they had been before, and he said,

"Listen to me. I have shown you all that is in the world, and what lies ahead of you. But remember, you must stay in the forest, you must not leave your dear grandfather until you have repaid all the love and care he has given you."

And with that the sun-god vanished away, leaving the brothers rubbing their eyes.

Well now, in the forest, besides the old man and his grandsons, there lived a tribe of goblins, hairy little

creatures known as vookodlaks, whose greatest wish it was to get rid of the sun and live in darkness. These goblins hated the old man and the boys, because they tended the sacred fire at the sun's shrine and kept it burning even at night, so that there was always a light in the forest.

It happened that the king of the vookodlaks had been hiding behind a tree, listening while the sun-god talked to the boys. And when they turned homeward, to tell their grandfather what they had seen and heard, the king of the vookodlaks scurried away to a muddy, murky, bushy part of the wood where he lived with all his tribe of ugly, dark, hairy, spiteful, brawling goblins.

"Hearken, you three," he said, picking out three goblin brothers, "follow those boys, stay with them, and, whatever you do, don't let them remember what the sun-god told them to do."

So the three goblins followed the three brothers, buzzing like a whole nestful of hornets, making it almost impossible to think. And the outcome of that was that by the time the boys reached the hut where they lived with their grandfather, they had clean forgotten what the sun-god told them to do. But they told their grandfather that they had seen the god, and that he had taken them to the mountain-top.

"And what did the great Daybog say to you?" the old man asked Martin.

As Martin stood scratching his head, one of the goblins sneaked up behind him and whispered, "Say, 'He told me I should be the richest man in the world.'"

As he could think of nothing else, Martin repeated this to his grandfather. Directly he did so, the goblin hopped into his pocket, and curled up there.

Then the old man turned to Mihal and said, "What did the great Daybog tell you, my child?"

Mihal could not remember either. But another goblin tiptoed up to him and whispered, "Tell him the sun-god promised that you would be the mightiest warrior in the world."

This seemed good advice to Mihal, so he repeated it, word for word. And the moment he did so, the second goblin jumped into his pocket, and there stayed.

Now the old man turned to his youngest grandson, Yanek. "And what did the sun-god tell you, my child?"

"Tell him the sun-god promised that you would be the wisest of men," whispered the third goblin.

But Yanek took no notice of the goblin's prompting, he gave it a kick, and said,

"I can't remember what the sun-god told me, Grandfather."

The little goblin slunk back to the king of the vookodlaks and confessed his failure. But the king grabbed him by his horns, beat him and thumped him, and said, "Go back to that boy and keep pestering him. Don't let him ever remember what the sun-god told him, or it will be the worse for you." So the little goblin went back and followed Yanek about, buzzing and bothering.

Meanwhile the other two goblins were hard at work changing the natures of Martin and Mihal. For Martin's goblin never let him rest unless he was at work fetching honey, or setting up more hives, or buying and selling, making himself richer and richer. And Mihal's goblin nagged at him to go off in search of weapons and warfare. "What is the use of staying here in the forest?" both goblins kept muttering and twittering.

But Yanek, the youngest grandson, tried and tried to remember what the sun-god had told him to do. At the end of three days he went to his grandfather, and said,

"Grandfather, I am going to climb the mountain and find a place where I can get some peace and quiet. And I shan't come back until I remember what the great Daybog said."

This news made the old man very sad, for he loved Yanek the best of his three grandsons.

"Oh, my dear boy! I may be dead by the time you come back."

But Yanek said, "I have thought about it, Grandfather, and I think it is right for me to go."

So the old man let him go, but with a heavy heart. And the little goblin followed Yanek up the mountain until they reached a high, lonely place where a waterfall ran down into a deep pool. Here Yanek sat down to think, and the goblin sat behind him.

Weeks went by and months went by.

Meantime Martin was becoming richer and richer, while Mihal spent all his time hunting and plundering. Neither of them paid any heed to the poor old grand-father, who had to tend the sacred fire all on his own. At last one day Martin said to Mihal,

"Why don't we get rid of the old man? He eats our food and provides nothing. You have plenty of weapons —why don't you kill him, then I can use his old hut to keep bees in." For Martin had built himself a handsome new house.

Mihal turned pale at the thought of killing his grandfather, but Martin kept on at him until he said, "Well, let us wait until he is asleep, and then we will burn down his hut. That won't be as bad as killing him outright."

So they did that. They waited until the old man was asleep and set fire to his hut. Then they hurried far away, so as not to have to listen to his cries.

The crackle of the flames woke the old man, and he tried to open his door. When he found that it was locked, he understood what his grandsons had done, and he sat down and wept for their hardness of heart. Then he quietly prepared to die.

Meanwhile Yanek, up on the mountain, was no nearer remembering what the sun-god had told him, because

the little goblin kept pestering
and distracting him every minute
of the time, turning somersaults,
sliding down the waterfall, buzzing
and chattering. At last Yanek knelt
down and prayed,

"Oh, great Daybog, lord of the sun,
please help me to remember what
you said!"

Directly he had done praying he
looked up, and there was the sun-god
standing beside him.

"Well, you are a stupid boy! I told
you to stay with your grandfather
till you had repaid the love and care
he has given you. And here I find
you, up on the mountain, doing no
good to anybody. I thought you were
wiser than your brothers, but I begin
to think you are the fool of the
family! Now, hurry home before it
is too late."

And the sun-god flung his golden
cloak round his shoulders and
vanished.

Yanek was very much ashamed.
But he thought, "Well, I'll go home
to grandfather directly. I'll just take
a drink, then I'll be off."

He knelt down by the pool. The
little goblin, who was

terribly afraid of what the king of the vookodlaks would
do to him if Yanek went home to look after his grandfather, gave him a great push. Yanek fell into the deep
pool and was drowned.

At first the little goblin was glad to be rid of his
charge. But then he began to be rather sorry. For he had
had a peaceful life of it with Yanek, up on the mountain.
He became sadder and sadder; presently he began to cry
and wail, then to scream and bellow with grief. His two
brothers, one in Martin's pocket and one in Mihal's,
heard their brother's cries and wondered what was
happening. At last they could stand it no longer. They
jumped down and ran to see what could be the matter
with him.

No sooner had the goblins left them than Martin and
Mihal stood still, pierced to the heart with a dreadful
guilt. They looked at each other in horror, and both
cried out,

"Brother! What have we done? Let us fly home and
save Grandfather!"

They flew home and found the blazing hut just about
to fall down. Mihal beat away the burning logs with his

club while Martin rushed in and picked up the old man. They laid him on the cool grass and bathed his forehead.

"Forgive us! Please forgive us, dear Grandfather!"

Slowly the old man opened his eyes.

"You are already forgiven, my children, or you would not be here. But now I must go; I cannot stay with you any longer."

And he rose to his feet and walked slowly away from them, up the mountain. Martin and Mihal followed him, frightened and wondering. The old man went higher and higher, along paths they had never seen before. At last they came to the topmost ridge of the mountain, and there lay a great field of cloud ahead of them. And on the white cloud floated a pink cloud, and on the pink cloud rose a glass mountain. And on the glass mountain stood a golden castle with a flight of steps leading to it. Inside the castle sat the great Daybog and his noble guests, drinking wine from golden cups.

Somebody sat on the steps of the castle weeping, with his face hidden in his hands.

The old man called, across the white cloud and the pink cloud.

"What is the trouble, my child?"

The weeper lifted his head, and they saw that it was Yanek.

"The sun-god won't let me into his palace, Grandfather," he answered, "because I did wrong to leave you."

Tears ran down the old man's cheeks when he heard that. He turned to Martin and Mihal and said to them, "Go back to the forest, my children, live rightly, and never let the sacred fire go out. I am going to help Yanek."

Martin and Mihal were very frightened.

"Grandfather, come back! You cannot walk on a cloud!"

But he was gone already, walking across the white cloud, and then across the pink cloud. He climbed the glass mountain and the golden steps. Then he and Yanek embraced one another, weeping for joy to be together again. The old man took Yanek by the hand, led him up to the castle door, and knocked.

Martin and Mihal, gazing from the mountain-top, saw the door fly open. The sun-god came forth, stretched out his hands, and welcomed grandfather and grandson into his golden home.

But Martin and Mihal went slowly down the mountain, and slowly back to the forest. Nor could they ever again find the paths they had taken that day. For the rest of their lives they lived in the forest. They married, had children, and tended the sacred fire. And so did their sons and grandsons after them.

As for the three goblins, they crept back to the king of the vookodlaks and he beat them all, and made them stand on their heads in the mud for three years and thirty days.

THE REED GIRL

There was once a king who decided that it was time for his son to marry. But the young man, when asked about it, said that if he must marry he would not take any poor skeleton of a girl, but that his wife must be the most beautiful creature on the whole round of the earth.

"Well, my son, but where is she to be found?"

"Perhaps the wise woman will know."

So they asked the wise woman.

"She lives far from here," said the wise woman. "As far as from here to there, and from there back."

"Where is that, then, mother?"

"You have heard of the Black Sea, perhaps? In the seventy-fourth island of the Black Sea, right in the middle, are hidden three reeds. It will be very hard to find them, for there is such a darkness on the islands of the Black Sea that a spoon might stand up in it. Moreover those three reeds are guarded by a witch whose life will end when they are cut down. But in one of those reeds is hidden a girl on whom the starry sky would gaze with smiles, for she is the most beautiful creature on the whole round of the earth."

"Very well," said the king's son, when he had heard all this from root to branch, "I will go in search of that Reed Girl."

And he saddled a horse and set off, over forty-nine kingdoms and beyond the Operentsia Sea, until he came to a hut where lived an old woman.

"Old mother, can you tell me where the Reed Girl is to be found?"

"No I cannot," said the old woman. "But I will call my servant who will take you to my sister; maybe she can help you." And she called, "Here, Mitsi, Mitsi!"

The king's son followed Mitsi, who was a small mouse with very long whiskers. So they came to a hut where another old woman lived.

"Old mother, can you tell me where the Reed Girl is to be found?"

"No, my son, but I will call my servant Pitsi to take you to my sister; maybe she will know."

Pitsi, who was a dove-white squirrel, took the king's son to the hut of the third old woman.

"Good day, dear old mother."

"It is a good thing you addressed me so politely, or I should have eaten you. What are you doing in this strange land, where even the birds do not fly?"

"I am looking for the Reed Girl."

"If you wore iron boots on your feet, you would wear out twelve pairs of them before you found her! You need a horse that has sucked dragon's milk and eaten glowing coals."

"Where can I find such a horse?"

"Happily for you," said the old woman, "I see three golden hairs growing on your head. Some fairy must have been in love with your father. Climb the high mountain behind my hut and strike the three golden hairs with this latch-string."

So the king's son climbed the mountain, pulled out his three golden hairs, and struck them with the latch-string. A fiery cloud rushed towards him, and down from it leaped the horse that had sucked dragon's milk and eaten glowing coals. The latch-string became a marvellous saddle, made of fur, with diamond buttons and silver embroidery.

"Climb on my back then, dear master," said the horse. "Shall I go as fast as a whirlwind, as fast as thought, or as fast as a bird?"

"Go as you choose, dear horse."

"Very well; but, as we are going to the islands where

there is such a darkness that a spoon might stand up in it, we must first go to the bright home of the sun and ask for one of his rays."

So they flew across the sky until they came to the doors of the world where two bearded wolves mount guard. These would not let the travellers pass without payment of two pounds of flesh, so the king's son cut off his hand and threw it to them.

Then the horse carried the king's son to the bright home of the Sun, the windswept isle of Bujan. Here they met Zora-djevojka, the Dawn Maiden, the Sun's beloved daughter. She gave the king's son honey to eat, and played to him on a golden zither, whose strings she brushed with a silver feather. Her music was so beautiful that his hand grew again from the stump. Then the Dawn Maiden gave him one of the Sun's burning rays; she wound it up like a ribbon and put it in a box which she hung round his neck. The king's son mounted his horse again, and they rode on for seven days, until they came to the islands of the Black Sea, where there is such darkness that a spoon might stand up in it. Now he opened his box and took out the sun's ray. It gave light, but only to him; not a created soul in the world could see him. He found the spot where the three reeds were growing and at a single blow cut down all three with his sword. When he did so a bitter cry was heard, and black blood flowed from the reed-stumps; this was the death-cry of the witch who guarded the reeds, and the blood was hers.

Quickly the king's son mounted his horse again and rode back over forty-nine kingdoms. But, as he rode, a

terrible curiosity began to rise up in him and prick him like a gimlet. He longed and longed to know if there really were girls inside the reeds. So at last, when he could not bear it any longer, he stopped and split one of the reeds with his dagger.

Out came a beautiful girl, fair as a pearl. But she sank on the ground calling out, "Water! Water! Give me a drop of water, only a drop, or I shall surely die."

One drop of water is not much to ask, but the king's son had none at all. So the poor girl grew paler and paler, her head dropped to the ground, and she died.

Then the king's son was so sorry for what he had done that he would willingly have died too, if it would have brought her back to life.

He dug a grave with his sword and buried the poor girl, planting the split reed above her; from it sprang a rose-bush with one black bloom. A bitter weeping was heard from the two reeds that remained, and the king's son thought,

"*I* caused the death of that poor girl; I broke off the flower and planted it in the garden of death." But if he had wept his soul away, it would have made no difference; so he mounted his horse and rode on.

But now again a wicked curiosity rose up in him, to know what was inside the second reed. At last he could resist the devil's prompting no longer; he drew his dagger and split the reed. Another girl came out, white as a pearl, crying, "Water! Water! Give me a drop of water, only a drop, or I shall die."

But the king's son had no drop of water to give her, and she drooped and died. At that the king's son was so sorry that he nearly died himself. But the harm was done. So he dug a grave with his sword, laid the poor girl in it, and planted the split reed above her. From it sprang a beautiful rose-bush which blossomed with black flowers. And a grievous weeping came from the last of the three reeds.

The king's son mounted his horse and rode on. Once more a terrible curiosity overcame him, to know what the third girl looked like. He took out the last reed— looked at it—was going to split it, but his horse reached back and snatched the reed from him. So they flew, until they reached the shores of a lake.

By the water's edge the king's son split the last reed, and a beautiful girl came out, so beautiful that her like has never been seen before or since. She cried, "Water! Water! Give me a drop, only a drop, or I shall surely die!"

So he made haste, and gave her water to drink in his helmet. They embraced and kissed, saying, "I am yours, and you are mine."

Then the king's son took her home to his father's palace, and they were married, and lived happily for many years.

THE KING WHO DECLARED WAR
ON THE ANIMALS

Once there was a poor young nobleman who had nothing in the world but a ruined castle in the forest, a horse, and a hound. So he was obliged to go hunting every day, in order to get his food. However he looked after his animals with great care, brushing and combing them every evening, giving them the same food as he had himself, and chopping wood to make a fire so that they should be warm at night. In consequence of this they loved him dearly.

One day the young lord went hunting with his hound in a densely thicketed part of the forest. He tied his horse to a tree outside this bushy patch and left him grazing.

Presently a fox came by and stopped to admire the horse.

"My word, brother, you seem fat and glossy! Your

master must look after you well."

"Indeed he does," said the horse. "Everything he has, I share."

"May I sit here for a while and keep you company?" asked the fox.

"By all means," replied the horse politely. So the fox sat down by him and chatted until the young lord came back with a stag which he had shot. He was rather astonished to see the fox, and raised his gun, at which the fox exclaimed,

"Don't shoot, my dear sir! Rather, take me into your service, and I'll keep an eye on your horse for you while you are off hunting. Good gracious! What a risky thing to leave a horse tied up here, when there are so many wolves and bears in the forest!"

The young lord thought this was sensible advice; he allowed the fox to come home with him, running alongside his hound. And when they arrived back at the ruined castle the fox was given a share of the supper and a place by the fire. "I certainly am in luck!" she thought.

Next day while the young lord went hunting the fox kept watch. Presently a hungry bear came along and began to sniff round the frightened horse.

"Hey, you bear! Leave the horse alone!" called out the fox. "If you will only sit down patiently and wait, our master, who is the most generous man in the world, will certainly give you a good supper when he comes back. Isn't that so, horse?"

"Yes indeed," said the horse, who was sweating with anxiety. "Everything he has, we share."

So the bear sat down and waited, and when the young

lord returned he was persuaded to take
the bear into his service. The bear had
supper and a bed for the night, and next
morning he helped the fox mount guard
over the horse.

While they sat and chatted, a mouse ran
up to them.

"Be off!" shouted the bear. "Can't you
see you are making the horse nervous?"

"Oh, kind sirs! Please let me stay with
you! Life is so dreadfully hard in the forest
these days, and you all look so well-fed and
contented."

"But what can *you* do for our master?"
said the bear in disgust.

"Oh, I daresay I can make myself useful in some way," replied the mouse. "It isn't everyone who can go through a keyhole, after all."

So when the young lord came back he was persuaded to take the mouse, too, into his service.

Next day a mole asked to be allowed to join them.

"Really!" said the fox. "I fail to see what use a miserable little blind mole can be!"

"Oh, you'd be surprised how much I can do," said the mole. "Why, I and a few of my friends can plough up a field as fast as two men and two teams of horses."

So the mole was permitted to go home with them and share their food and fire.

Next day a great buzzard asked if she might join them.

"I am extremely strong," she said. "I can pick up a horse and rider in my talons and carry them right across the forest."

And a wild cat came by.

"I can amuse you all with my purring and my playful ways."

So the cat and the buzzard were added to their company, and the young lord looked after them all, fed them and kept them warm. And they were all exceedingly fond of him.

But one day when the lord was off hunting the fox said:

"Friends, *we* are all happy and contented, but our master sometimes seems rather sad and downcast. It has come into my mind that he needs a wife, one of his own kind, to keep him company. Where can one be found?"

"The other day when I flew over the palace of the king," said the buzzard, "I noticed that he has a very beautiful daughter. Why don't I fetch her to be our master's wife?"

This seemed a good plan to them all.

The buzzard flew to the king's palace, waited, perching in an oak tree, until the princess came out for her evening stroll, and then picked her up and carried her back to the forest, holding her as carefully as if she were made of rose petals.

The young lord was overjoyed to see what a beautiful wife his friends had found for him. Since he looked after her as carefully as he did the rest, the princess too was happy to share their life in the forest.

But her father the king was angry and sad at the loss of his daughter; he asked a wise woman to find out what had become of the princess.

The wise woman filled a bowl with water and looked into it. Then she said,

"Your daughter is living in the forest with a young nobleman. If you will give me half your treasure I will fetch her back for you."

"Very well," said the king.

So the wise woman, taking a whip in her hand, seated herself on a small carpet and lashed it with the whip until it rose in the air and carried her to the forest. There she saw the princess, walking outside the ruined castle with all the animals keeping guard over her.

"Would you like to listen to some fine stories?" said the wise woman. "I know stories about heroes, stories about magicians, stories about birds and beasts, summer and winter, the sun, the moon, and the stars."

The princess was very fond of stories, so she was eager to listen to the wise woman.

"Sit beside me on my carpet, then, and I will tell you about the golden apple and the nine peahens."

But when the princess sat down beside her on the carpet, the wise woman snatched up her whip and lashed the carpet with it; next minute they were far away, flying back to the king's palace. And the king shut his daughter in a tower, lest she be stolen again.

The poor young lord was grief-stricken at the loss of his bride, and the animals were very downcast in sympathy.

"Friends, we must get her back," said the fox. "You, cat, must go and play about in the garden of the tower, but don't let the princess's women catch you."

So the striped cat made her way to the garden of the

tower. There she played most beautifully, pouncing on leaves and grasses as they blew in the wind, pretending to chase her own tail. "Oh, the pretty creature!" exclaimed the waiting-women. "Let us catch her to amuse our mistress." But, try as they would, they were unable to catch the cat.

"Let me out, just for a moment," called the princess, who was watching from the window. "I am sure she will come to me."

"Only for a moment, then," said the women. "For if the king your father knew, it would be as much as our place was worth."

So they undid the door and the princess stepped into the garden. And the buzzard, who had been waiting hidden in the branches of an oak tree, swooped down, picked her up as carefully as if she were made of rose petals, and carried her back to the forest.

The king was furious at being tricked again, and by nothing more than a pair of animals, at that.

In his rage he declared war on the whole animal tribe, swearing that he would exterminate the lot of them, and recapture his daughter at the same time. So he collected a huge army with men, horses, and guns, and, following the wise woman's directions, set out for the forest.

"Now what are we going to do?" said the bear.

"We must defend ourselves as best we can," said the fox. "Each one of you must call as many companions as possible. I myself can summon five hundred foxes. How about you?" she asked the bear.

"Oh, I think I can count on about a hundred," said the bear.

"And you, dear cat?"

"About eight hundred," said the cat.

"And you, little mouse?"

"Eight thousand, for sure."

"And you, friend mole?"

"Oh, three thousand at least."

"And you, O great buzzard?"

"I fear not more than two or three hundred."

So each animal went to fetch his companions, while the fox made a plan of battle.

The king's army marched until nightfall; then they made camp. But during the night the mice invaded their camp and gnawed through all the halters, saddle-girths, and reins, while the bears, foxes, and cats growled and howled around the outskirts of the camp with a sound fearful enough to make your blood run cold. The king's horses, finding their halters cut through, made off in

terror. Next day not a horse was to be seen.

"You must continue on foot, then," said the angry king to his soldiers. "You will have to pull the great guns yourselves, since there are no horses."

So they went on with great difficulty. Next night the mice came again, and gnawed through the soldiers' belts and sword-straps, so they had no means of keeping their swords and their breeches on. Moreover the moles dug hundreds of tunnels under their line of march. When they tried to stumble on, the heavy guns sank up to their barrels in the ground; meanwhile the buzzards hovered overhead, hurling down great rocks on the struggling men.

"Oh, well, let us turn back," said the king at last. "I can see God himself must be against us, since I have declared war on the animals. I will just have to give up my daughter!"

So he went back to his palace and sent a message telling the princess that she and her husband were forgiven. And they came to the palace with all their animals and lived happily together for many years.

THE VENETIAN PRINCESS

There was a Venetian princess, Roksanda, who was said to be marvellously beautiful, and the Tsar Doushan of Serbia wished to seek her hand in marriage. But when he sent his ambassador to see if she were indeed as beautiful as men told, the Venetians would only show him the princess at nightfall, in an unlighted room. Luckily the ambassador had with him his master's ring; by the light of the diamond in it, he was able to see Roksanda, and he returned to tell Doushan that she was indeed a girl on whom the heavens might smile. So Doushan sent to her father King Michael to know when he might come to fetch her, and how many svats—how many armed lords—he might bring with him.

King Michael sent word:

"Come when you choose, dear friend, and bring as many svats as you please. Only do not, I beg, bring those two trouble-makers, your nephews Peter and Vankashin, the Voinovitchs.''

So Tsar Doushan called together all his svats and set forth. When the brilliant wedding procession passed through the field of Kossovo and by the castle of the Voinovitchs, the king's two nephews said sadly to one another,

"Our uncle must be angry with us, or surely he would have invited us to go with him? May a hundred evils befall him who has spoken against us! Our Tsar is going among the false Venetians. Alas, what will become of him without us to defend him?''

Then their mother said, "Oh, my sons, send and fetch your youngest brother Milosh, who guards the sheep in the mountains. The Tsar has not heard tell of him and won't know him; maybe he will be allowed to join the wedding procession.''

So Milosh was sent for, and he gladly agreed to go. "If I were not willing to aid our dear uncle, it would be a strange day indeed!''

He put on a white silk shirt, all embroidered with gold; over the shirt he placed three thin, elegant ribbons; then a scarlet velvet waistcoat adorned with thirty gold buttons; and then his golden armour. Over it all he flung the coarse black cloak of a Bulgar shepherd, and placed on his head a Bulgar's black fur cap with high points, so that his own mother would not have known him; and he took his weapons and mounted the famous horse Koulash, on whom Peter had fastened a bearskin so that he would not be recognized.

When Milosh caught up with the gay procession of

knights, they hailed him:

"Where are you going, little Bulgar?"

"I have been serving the Turks, and am looking for better employment. May I join you?"

"Indeed you may!"

So Milosh joined the procession. Now, being a shepherd, he was accustomed to doze at noontime, and so he fell asleep, and his hand relaxed on the rein. The great horse Koulash galloped forward to join the Tsar's horses, and fell into step with them. Milosh awoke then, and reined back his horse: the great Koulash bounded up to the height of three lances, fire burst from his mouth, and blue flame from his nostrils. All the svats were astonished, and said among themselves, "Such a horse has never been seen, save in the stable of the Voinovitchs!

It is strange that it should belong to that black Bulgar."

Now they came to King Michael's white city of Ledyen and raised their tents beneath its walls. And King Michael sent a haughty message:

"Listen, O Serbian Tsar! Our champion waits in the valley, and you or one of your svats must overcome him before you may take the princess Roksanda!"

But none of Tsar Doushan's svats was willing to fight the Venetian champion.

Then Doushan was so cast down that his moustaches drooped to his shoulders. He exclaimed, "Woe is me, if I only had my two darling nephews I should not lack a champion."

"O mighty Tsar, have I your leave to fight this combat?" said Milosh.

"Indeed, you are welcome, O youthful Bulgar! But I an afraid there is little chance of your defeating King Michael's champion."

Milosh leaped on to the great horse Koulash and rode off, with his lance turned backward over his shoulder. King Doushan called,

"O my son, do not carry your lance so, or the proud Venetians will mock you!"

But Milosh replied, "O my
Tsar, do you look after your
own dignity, and I will look
after mine."

All the Venetian ladies laughed
as Milosh approached.

"What a champion to send
forth! Look at the ugly black
Bulgar! Why, he is not even
wearing respectable clothes!"

But Milosh reversed his lance
and flung it so hard that it
pinned the Venetian champion to
the gate of the city; he struck off
the champion's head and threw
it in Koulash's nosebag. The Tsar
Doushan was overjoyed.

"For this, my son, I shall give
you much honour!"

Now the Venetians sent another
message:

"In the meadow are three
horses, each with a flaming

sword point upright on its saddle. Before you can take the princess Roksanda, you or your champion must leap at one bound over these horses and flaming swords."

But none of the Serbian svats was willing to attempt such a feat. Then Milosh said,

"O my Tsar, have I your leave to try?"

"Certainly you may, dear son! But before you go, won't you please take off that clumsy Bulgarian cloak (may God punish the stupid tailor who made it)?"

But Milosh replied, "Sit in peace, mighty Tsar, and drink your cool wine. If a sheep finds her wool too heavy, there is no sheep in her, nor any wool."

He approached the three horses and, dancing first on one foot and then on the other, ran like a deer, leapt over the three horses, over the flaming swords, and alighted on the saddle of his own horse, the great Koulash. Then he rode in triumph to the Tsar.

Now King Michael sent a message:

"In front of the king's palace are three beautiful girls. Unless you can guess which of the three is Roksanda, neither you nor your svats shall leave this place alive!"

The king at once called his ambassador. But he declared that he would be unable to recognize Roksanda, after having seen her for such a short time, and that only by the light of his master's ring.

"Alas!" exclaimed the Tsar. "Must we return without the bride, to the shame of our people?"

Then Milosh said, "Have I your leave, O Tsar, to try to guess which is the princess?"

"Indeed you have, O darling son! But I fear there is small chance that you will guess correctly, never having seen Roksanda!"

"Do not worry, O glorious Tsar! When I was a shepherd I could easily tell, out of three hundred lambs born in a night, which lamb belonged to which mother. It will be easy to tell Roksanda from her likeness to her brothers."

"Go, then, my darling son! If you guess right, I shall give you the whole land of Skender."

Milosh went to where the three girls were waiting. He swept off his black fur cap and his heavy cloak, revealing the scarlet velvet and golden armour which had been hidden beneath. Laying his cloak on the ground, he threw on it gold rings and pearls and precious stones. Then he unsheathed his sword and said to the girls,

"Let the princess Roksanda roll up her sleeves and collect these precious things. But if either of the others should dare to touch them, I shall cut off her arms at the elbows!"

Two of the girls were terrified and looked pleadingly at the third; so Roksanda gathered up the precious stones. The other girls would have fled then, but Milosh took their hands and gently led all three into the presence of the Tsar. One of the two companions went with Roksanda to attend her; the other agreed to marry Milosh.

Now the wedding procession started homeward.

But in the middle of the plain of Kossovo Milosh came to take leave of the Tsar.

"May God be with you, my dear uncle! My way lies to the right."

Only now did the Tsar discover that the Bulgar was none other than his nephew, Prince Milosh Voinovitch.

"Oh, my darling boy! Happy is the mother who gave birth to you, and happy the uncle who has such a courageous nephew! Why in the world did you not reveal yourself sooner?"

Woe to him who overlooks his own relations!

THE PEAR TREE

Long ago, near the beginning of things, when the earth was almost all covered in forest, God sent down the angel Gabriel to see how people were getting along, and if they had enough to eat. There were three poor brothers living at that time who owned nothing in the world but one pear tree. This tree, though, was as beautiful as a miracle, for it was very tall, and bore leaves, flowers, and fruit, all at the same time; the leaves were green as emerald, the flowers white as snow, and the pears fine, large, and glossy, big as your two fists put together. And the tall tree arched over at the top in a graceful curve like a shepherd's crook, as if it were looking down to admire itself.

Well, the angel Gabriel disguised himself as a poor beggar and walked through the forest until he came to this pear tree. The eldest brother was lying under the tree, keeping guard over it to make sure nobody stole the fruit, while the other two took some pears to market.

"Oh, kind sir," Gabriel besought him, "I am so tired and hungry from travelling through the forest. Could you spare me just one of your beautiful pears?"

"Certainly, poor old man," said the eldest brother. And he picked a basketful of the pears and gave them to Gabriel. "These are from my share of the fruit," he said, "for I can't give you the pears that belong to my brothers."

Next day Gabriel returned to the tree. This time the middle brother was keeping guard over it while the other two carried some of the fruit to market.

"Oh, kind sir," begged Gabriel, "could you give me a pear or two, just to keep a poor old traveller from dying of hunger?"

"Willingly, you poor old fellow," said the middle brother, and he gave Gabriel some choice pears. "These are mine," he said, "for naturally I can't give you pears from my brothers' share."

On the third day Gabriel came again to the tree and found the youngest brother keeping watch. And he, too, when asked, gave the angel some fruit from his share, explaining that he could not give away his brothers' pears.

Next day Gabriel took the form of a monk and returned to the tree; this time he found all three brothers lying under it in the shade and talking together, while the white blossom fell on them like snow. For it was Sunday and there was no market.

"Come with me, poor brothers," Gabriel said to them,

"and I will give you a better life." So, very much astonished, they followed him through the forest.

Presently they came to a great waterfall.

Here Gabriel said to the eldest brother, "Because of your kindness to the poor traveller, you can make any wish and it will be granted."

"In that case," said the eldest brother, "I wish that this waterfall should all be turned to wine, and that the wine should all belong to me."

"Your wish is granted," said Gabriel, making the sign of the cross with his staff. And on that very instant the waterfall was turned to red wine, and there were men with staves, making casks, men stoking furnaces to make bottles, men collecting the wine. "All this is yours," Gabriel told the eldest brother. "See you put it to good use." And he went on his way with the other two.

Next they came to a clearing in the forest where they saw a great flock of doves.

"Now it is your turn for a wish," Gabriel said to the second brother. "Ask for anything you like, because you gave some of your fruit to the poor beggar."

"In that case," said the second brother, "I wish all these doves could be turned to a herd of cattle, and I wish they belonged to me."

Directly he spoke, Gabriel made the sign of the cross, and all the doves were turned into cattle. Moreover there were herdsmen looking after them, and girls milking them, and women churning butter and making cheese.

"All this is for you," Gabriel said to the second brother. "You will be able to earn yourself a proper living."

And he went on his way with the youngest brother until they came to a long glade in the forest.

"Now," said Gabriel to the youngest brother, " it is your turn for a wish. What would you like?"

The youngest brother said, "I should like a good Christian girl for a wife."

Gabriel scratched his head at that.

"You ask a most awkward thing," he said. "There are only three such girls in the world. One is married already, one has declared that she will never take a husband, and the third has two suitors after her as it is. However, we shall see what we can do."

So he took the youngest brother to the village where the good Christian girl lived. Her name was Militsa. When they entered her house they saw that the table was already covered with gold and silver gifts from the other two suitors, with woven cloth, silks and velvets, and embroidered slippers and carved ornaments. All the youngest brother could put down for his gift was a basket of pears.

"What kind of a present is that?" exclaimed the girl's father scornfully.

But Militsa had seen the youngest brother and liked his looks.

"Let it be decided this way," she said to her father. "Let each of them plant a vine, and I will marry the man whose vine first bears fruit."

So this was done, and on the very next day fine grapes were found hanging on the youngest brother's vine. The girl's father could make no further objection, so the two of them were married directly, and went to live in the forest.

Gabriel went back and told God what he had done for the three brothers.

"Are you sure you did right?" said God.

"Of course I did!" said the angel Gabriel.

"Well," said God, "we shall see. Leave them for a year, and then go back to find out how they are getting on."

At the end of a year Gabriel went to visit the eldest brother. As before, he disguised himself in beggar's clothes, and hobbled into the village which had sprung up around the river of wine. There were inns and stalls, shops, swings, and merry-go-rounds; all the money from these things went to the eldest brother. So Gabriel knocked at the door of his fine large house and asked for a cup of wine.

"The idea! If I gave a cup of wine to every vagabond who came whining to my door, how do you imagine I would make a living?" exclaimed the eldest brother. "Be off, before I call the constables!"

"Humph," said the angel Gabriel at this, and he made the sign of the cross. Directly he did so, the whole village, shops, inns, stalls, and people, and the river of wine, all vanished away; nothing remained but the waterfall dashing over its crag. "That good luck was not for you," Gabriel told the eldest brother. "You were better as you were before. Go back to your pear tree!"

Then Gabriel went to visit the second brother, who was now running a great farm, with dairies, and butcheries where they sold meat, and tanneries where they sold boots and saddles and all kinds of things made out of leather. Gabriel knocked at the second brother's door and asked for a drink of milk.

"A likely thing it would be if I were to give a drink of milk to every beggar who passed through!" exclaimed the second brother. "Be off, before I set the dogs on you!"

"Humph," muttered Gabriel at this, and he made the sign of the cross. At once the farm, the cattle, the shops and stalls, houses and barns, men and women, vanished clean away. Nothing was left but a clearing in the forest and a flock of doves who rose up into the air, wheeled round, and flew off.

"That good luck was not for you. I can see you were better as you were before," Gabriel told the second brother. "Go back to your pear tree."

And he went on his way, scratching his head.

Now he came to the youngest brother, who was living in a tiny hut in the forest with his young wife Militsa. They were so poor that they had to grind up the bark of trees to make flour for their bread.

Gabriel knocked at the door and asked if they could give him a bed for the night and a bite to eat.

"Willingly," said Militsa, and she put a loaf of bark bread in the ashes to bake. And she gave Gabriel a mossy

stone to sit on, and a pillow of leaves. But, much to her surprise, when the bread was baked and she took it out, she found that it had turned to a beautiful large loaf of the finest wheat flour.

"God be thanked," she said to her husband, "now we have something better to offer our guest." And she put it before Gabriel on a wooden plate and gave him a wooden cup full of water. But when they came to drink they found the water had changed to wine. And in the morning, when they went outside their hut to speed the traveller on his way, they found that the poor little cabin had turned into a handsome mansion, with everything around it that they could possibly need. So they lived happily for many years.

Gabriel went back to heaven.

"What about the other two brothers?" asked God.

"Some people are best left alone," said Gabriel, and he looked down to where the eldest and the middle brother were lying peacefully under their beautiful tree, with its green leaves, and its glossy fruit, and the white blossom falling like snow.

THE SUN'S COUSIN

Once an elderly couple kept a mill in a lonely place, between forest and marsh. The miller was a hard, miserly man, who grudged even the husks of the corn that he ground. When the farmers came with their grain he asked as his fee one-half of the flour, and the half the farmer received would, as often as not, be full of dust and siftings. But since there was no other mill, people had to put up with such treatment.

The miller's wife was just as mean as her husband, but their daughter Neva was quite different; she was happy-natured and kind-hearted, sang all day at her work like a thrush, and was as beautiful as she was kind, with summer-blue eyes and hair the colour of the sun's rays at noon. Nor was this surprising, for she had been born on the shortest day of the year, which is the sun's birthday also. And therefore people said of her that she would be lucky, for things had begun to grow just as she appeared, buds started to sprout and birds to practise their spring songs. Moreover, when she was born, the vili, the fairies of the millstream, had dipped her in the drops that fell from the mill-wheel, so that all trouble should likewise fall away from her.

Well, one cold winter day an old woman came to the mill with a bag of corn to be ground. She came out of the marshes, and she was grey all over—grey hair, grey face, grey rags and tatters—and all mired and spattered, besides, from the marsh mud. Only her eyes shone very bright and sharp.

"What is your fee for grinding my corn?" she said to the miller.

"Half the flour it makes, old marshwife," said the miller.

"That is too much!" snapped the old woman. "It won't leave me enough for my yuletide cake."

"What is that to me?" said the miller, shrugging his shoulders. "Half the bag is my fee, take it or leave it."

The old woman shouldered her bag again, giving him a baleful look, and went muttering away.

But Neva the miller's daughter had overheard this talk and felt sorry for the old woman who wanted to bake her yuletide cake. So she ran down through the trees and caught up with the old woman just as she was about to start off across the marsh.

"Come again tomorrow, Granny, for my father and mother will have gone to market then and I shall be alone. I'll grind your corn for you and charge you nothing at all."

So the old wife came back next day with her bag of corn. And Neva waded into the ice-cold stream, opened the sluice, started up the mill-wheel, and ground the old woman's bag of corn.

"Thank you, my young lass," said the old woman. "Since you have been so kind to me I'll tell your fortune for you. When were you born?"

"On midwinter day, Granny."

Now this was no ordinary old woman. Her name was Mokosh, and she was the sun's foster-mother. For every year at midwinter the sun grows weak and pale, and he sinks down into the marshes to spend the long winter night there, and Mokosh, the old witch, his foster-mother, nurses him until he is strong again, with herbs and spells and incantations. Besides being the sun's foster-mother, Mokosh could foretell the future, and she could change herself into any form she pleased, bird or fish or snake of the swamp.

So she looked at Neva's hand and into her eyes, and told her,

"You will be lucky, for the sun is your kinsman, born in the same hour. And I'll tell him that it was due to your kindness that I was able to bake his birthday cake."

So she slung her bag over her shoulder and went away across the marshes.

From that day on, nothing about the mill went well unless Neva had a hand in it. Unless she kept a watch over the flour, rats ate it, unless she opened the sluice, the water would not drive the wheel. Whatever the miller and his wife did was all wasted labour. And soon they began to hate Neva, and to wish to be rid of her.

Presently it was summer, midsummer day, with the sun high and lordly in the sky. And old Mokosh came again to Neva.

"Now, my young lass, I have come to make your fortune in return for the kindness you did me," she said. "You must go to the city, for the princess of this land has lost her keys as she rode out in the meadows by the river, and she has sent all her people to hunt for them. And she has promised a reward to whosoever finds the keys: if it is a man, he is to marry the princess and be her husband and true love; if it is a maiden she will become the princess's first lady-in-waiting and sit at her left hand. You must go to the meadow and find the keys, and then the princess will make you her lady."

"But, Granny, how likely is it that I should find the keys, if all her people are out already hunting for them?"

"Don't argue with me, for I get very angry when I am crossed," snapped the old woman. "The keys are hidden under a clump of yellow flag that grows by the river, and if you will follow me I will lead you to them."

So old Mokosh changed herself to a moorhen and ran through the meadows to the town, and Neva followed her.

When they came near the princess's tower they saw a great number of people, all walking in the meadows, all searching for the princess's lost keys. And the princess herself sat up at the window of the tower, watching.

Mokosh, disguised as a moorhen, ran straight through all the people towards the clump of yellow flag, and Neva followed her. But on her way, she saw a noble knight, riding slowly through the meadows on a black horse. And Neva's heart began to fail her; she thought, "That knight is far more worthy to find the keys than I am."

At this moment the princess, looking from her window, saw Neva the poor miller's daughter going through her meadows. The princess turned and spoke to some of her menservants:

"Go", she said to them, "and drive that ragged girl away with your whips. I do not want such a one as that for my lady-in-waiting!"

But by the time the menservants had crossed the meadow Mokosh, still disguised as a moorhen, had led Neva straight to the clump of yellow flag, and there, shining below the leaves, lay the princess's keys. Neva picked them up. But her heart failed her again when she looked towards the tower, and at the high princess sitting by her window, all dressed in fur and silver. And just then the noble knight came near, on his black horse. For his heart had been taken by the sight of Neva, as hers with him, and he had followed her.

"*You* take the keys, stranger knight, and become the princess's husband and true love," said Neva, holding them out to him. "For I find I have no heart in me to become the princess's lady-in-waiting."

Now the princess's menservants came up with their whips and tried to drive Neva from the meadows, shouting, "Be off! The princess does not wish such as you to find her keys!"

At this the stranger knight grew angry, and he leaned down from his horse and lifted Neva on to the saddle. His great black horse made its way through the crowd

of menservants until he came alongside the princess's window. And he tossed the bunch of keys so that they flew sparkling through the air and landed in the princess's lap.

"Since you do not want the maiden, I am taking her for myself, gracious princess!" he called. "And I shall be her husband and true love." With that he spurred his horse, and rode away across the marshes to his castle, three long days' journey distant.

This knight was named Oleg Ban, and he was so poor that he had only a horse and two hounds, nine men to fight for him, nine maids, and a wooden fortress; but he was the bravest knight in the whole land. Neva's heart nearly burst within her for pride and joy at being chosen by such a noble knight. So they lived happily in his fortress for a month and a day, celebrating their wedding feast.

But the princess had been bitterly angered by Oleg's scorn, for she had hoped to marry him herself. She caused a great army to be collected, and she set off at the head of the army to punish Oleg Ban.

In the wooden fortress they were still feasting when the princess's army came in sight. Their swords and spears flashed, and a great cloud of arrows came flying, so that the air was black with them. The nine fighting men were wounded, and some of the nine maids, and Oleg Ban himself had a grievous wound.

Then the princess's soldiers began to batter at the doors of the wooden fortress with their axes.

"I will send for old Mokosh," Neva said. "Surely she will help us in this trouble."

And she sent off a turtle-dove to ask help from the old marshwife. Mokosh changed herself into a raven and flew back with the turtle-dove to perch on the ridge of the wooden fort.

"Can you aid us now, old Granny?" called Neva to the raven. "Unless you can, I fear there is no hope for us."

"Indeed I shall not help you," said the raven spitefully. "You have only yourself to thank for the plight you are in! If you had done as I said, and given the keys to the princess, you would now be dressed in silk, sitting at her left hand. Woe to those who disregard the advice of old Mokosh. Save yourselves, for I shall have nothing to do with you."

Oleg Ban became angry at that.

"Take no notice of the ill-omened bird!" he said. "We will open the gates and rush out upon the princess's men; if we must die, at least we will die bravely, and not begging for help from an old black scavenger."

And he went to bid his men unbar the doors.

Then Neva had a better idea; she looked up to heaven and saw the mighty sun travelling across the sky overhead, darting his gold rays down like arrows.

"Oh, my kinsman the Sun, will you not help me? Remember it was I who ground the flour for your birthday cake!"

The sun remembered, and he sent down his beams like a blessing on bright-headed Neva. But upon the raven that was Mokosh he frowned, and bade her take herself underground.

"Down with you into the marsh, you spiteful old foster-mother! Help me get rid of this rabble that is troubling my little cousin there in the wooden fortress!"

Mokosh could not refuse him; she sank under the earth, which opened to receive her.

Then the sun put forth all his power; he blazed and scorched, he struck down upon the princess's soldiers so that their helmets turned to molten brass on their heads, and their swords melted like candles in their hands. Each man died where he stood; they fell in their tracks without a sound. And as each man died, old Mokosh dragged him down by his feet into the swamp, so that without a stroke of battle the whole army vanished. And the angry princess, she, too, died where she sat on her horse; a boghole opened at her feet and she sank into it.

But Oleg Ban, and Neva, and their nine fighting men and nine maids, they were all safe under their wooden roof. And so, when the sun's rage had died away, they finished celebrating their wedding feast with great joy, and the sun himself came down to give away his little cousin to her bridegroom.

THE GOLDEN-FLEECED RAM AND
THE HUNDRED ELEPHANTS

There was once a young man called Marko who was lucky enough to own a very handsome ram with a golden fleece. Now it so chanced that the king of the country passed through Marko's village, and he saw the golden-fleeced ram and set his heart on it. But instead of setting about matters in a straightforward way and asking Marko if he would sell him the ram, or let him have it as a gift—which Marko might well have done, for he was a good-natured young man—the king asked the advice of his prime minister Milosu, who was Marko's uncle.

Milosu had always disliked his nephew, and he thought this would be a first-class chance to get rid of him and take his farm.

"Set the young man some impossible task," he said to the king. "Then when he fails you can chop his head off and take the ram."

The king listened to this bad advice.

He sent for Marko and told him, "You must plant me a vineyard and bring me wine from it in seven days. Otherwise I shall have your head cut off."

Poor Marko was very upset. He wandered out of the village and up the mountain, weeping and wondering what he could possibly do. When he had gone some distance from the houses he met a mysterious little girl, who suddenly appeared from behind a rock, and said,

"Why are you weeping, my brother?"

"Oh, leave me alone!" he snapped. "Go your way, in God's name. My trouble is nothing to do with you, and you certainly can't help me."

"Maybe I can, just the same," she said. "There's no harm in telling me." And she persisted until he said, "Oh, very well," and told her what was worrying him.

"Why, I think we can do something about that," said the little girl. "I don't think that is too much of a problem. Go back, have the vineyard marked out, and order it to be trenched in straight lines. Now take these twigs of basil, put them into a sack, and for seven nights you must sleep lying between the trenches of the vineyard, with your head pillowed on the sack."

And the mysterious little girl picked a bunch of the sweet mountain basil, with its grey leaves like smoke, and gave them to Marko. As he could think of no better plan, he did what she told him. He ordered the land to be dug and trenched, he put the basil-sprigs in a sack, and for seven nights slept between the trenches.

On the first morning he found the vines ready planted; on the second morning the leaves had begun to sprout;

on the third the vines had
grown tall; on the fourth morning
they were in flower; on the fifth morning
small grapes had begun to form; on the
sixth morning the grapes were large and
green; on the seventh morning the grapes
were ripe and ready for picking.

Since it was the golden-fleeced ram the king really wanted, he was not at all pleased when Marko came before him on the seventh day with a jug of sweet wine and a cluster of grapes in his handkerchief.

"Never mind," said the wicked uncle Milosu. "That plan didn't work, but now we'll find him something really impossible to do. Tell him to build a tower out of a hundred elephants' tusks."

Marko heard this order with despair. "Why," he thought, "in this country it is uncommon to see even one elephant; how can I ever expect to find a hundred?"

And he wandered out of the village and up the wild mountain, with tears running down his cheeks.

He had not gone very far when the mysterious little girl suddenly appeared again, from the dry gully of a mountain stream.

"Why are you weeping, my brother?"

"Oh, what use is it to tell you?" he said. "This time it is quite impossible that you should be able to help me."

"Oh well, you never know," said she. "In any case you might just as well relieve your mind by talking the

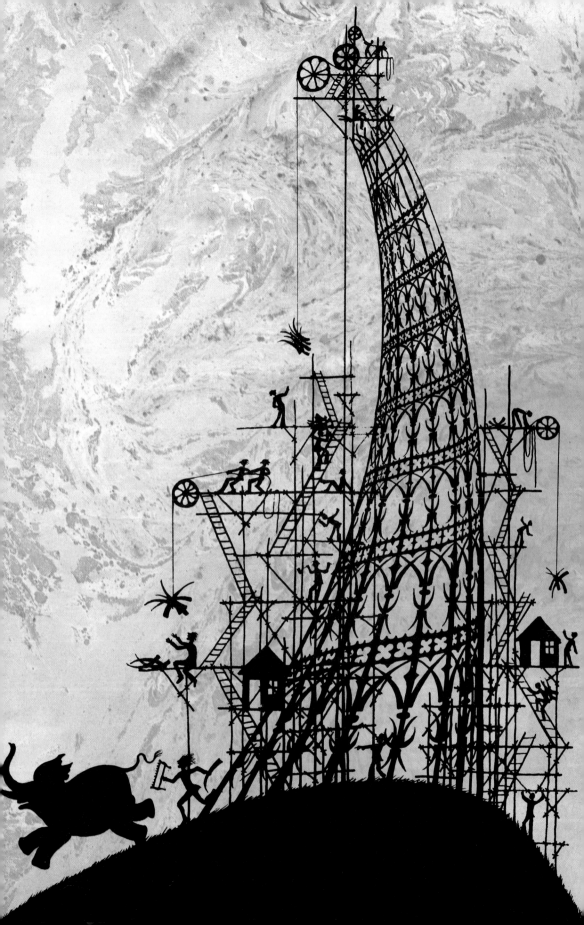

matter over."

So Marko told her that he had been ordered to build a tower out of elephants' tusks.

"Oh, I do not think that is an impossible task," said the mysterious child. "What you must do is this: go back to the king and ask for three hundred barrels of wine and three hundred barrels of brandy. Have men with oxen drag the barrels up the mountain to a lake with a narrow outlet. Pour all the wine and brandy into the lake, and make a dam so that it cannot escape. Then many elephants will come to drink from the lake, and they will become drunk and fall down. Have carpenters ready to cut off their tusks; then, at the spot where the tower is to be built, you must lie down and sleep for seven nights with your head pillowed on the sack of basil. On the seventh day the tower will be ready."

This time Marko believed the mysterious child; he went to the king and asked for three hundred barrels of wine and three hundred barrels of brandy, and for oxen to drag them up the mountain and men to dam up the lake.

Sure enough, when they had dammed the lake and poured in all the wine and brandy from the barrels, hundreds of elephants came hasting through the mountains, having smelt the liquor from many miles away. They came down to the verge of the lake, and drank and drank.

The wine and brandy made them joyful and they began to dance, waving their long trunks and fanning each other with their great ears. They trumpeted gaily, and the ground shook, so that the people in the king's city trembled and thought the mountain must be falling down.

Marko watched the elephants dance and he thought to himself, "Why should these happy creatures lose their tusks so that the king may have an ivory tower? What have they done to deserve such a fate?"

And he pulled out the keystone of the dam. Down rushed all the wine and brandy, straight down the side of the mountain so that the king, and his palace, and his wicked minister Milosu were all swept away. But the elephants went gaily dancing and trumpeting away over the mountains, through Roumania and Georgia, through Turkey, Iran, and Afghanistan, until they came to their native land. And Marko went with them, riding on the largest elephant.

As for the golden-fleeced ram, it escaped up the mountain, who knows where?

As for the mysterious little girl, she was never seen again.

THE GOOSE GIRL

One day God and St Peter were out taking the air together in the green countryside. St Peter walked along silently for a long distance. Then he suddenly burst out:

"It must be a fine thing to be God! My goodness, if I could only be God for a short time—even half a day!—then I'd be content to be St Peter for ever after!"

God smiled at that. "Very well, my dear Peter, if you are so set on it, your wish is granted. Be God until nightfall!"

They went on a little farther, and ahead of them they saw a village. A girl was coming in their direction, driving a flock of geese in front of her. She shooed all the geese into a meadow, left them, and started back towards the village again.

"Surely you aren't going to leave those geese unguarded?" St Peter said.

"Well, what? You don't expect me to stay with them today? It's a feast day!"

"But who will look after the geese?"

"God Almighty!" And off she ran.

"Well, Peter, you heard what she said," God told him. "I'm sorry you can't come with me to the village feast; I should have been delighted to take you—but then the geese might come to harm. You are God until nightfall, I'm afraid it's your job to protect them."

So Peter had to stay and mind the geese.

Never again did he wish to be God.

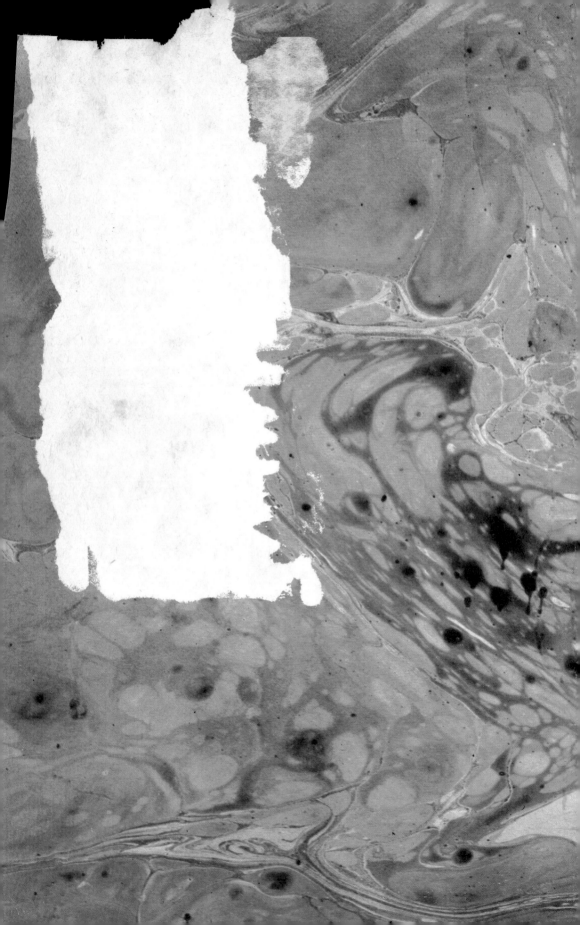